The

Ghost

Of

Tucker Hall

The Ghost Of Tucker Hall

The

Ghost

Of Tucker Hall

Stephen A Higgins

Platinum House
Publishing

Print Edition ISBN-13: 978-1-68096-016-7

For My Grandmother Joyce Higgins

The Ghost Of Tucker Hall

The Ghost Of Tucker Hall

Willie Lester

****

Into the night-shrouded swamp went Willie Lester, searching for the woman who had once told him she wasn't worthy of his love. From a far distance behind him he heard the shrill, demon-shrieking of that grinning idol of darkness, calling upon his gold-horned handmade beasts.

And in his ears reverberated the horrifying screams of Veronica Tucker from that secret cabin of evil, Satan's signature had been signed by the marks of cloven hoofs.

CHAPTER ONE

The Swamp Horror

In the middle of the night echoed the sound of a loud quivering scream. It lasted for two minutes, a scarlet thread of sound. Then it stopped, the whisper of wind-stirred frondescence and the piercing discordant of the crickets, shrieking an obbligato to terror.

Veronica Tucker was cold and motionless, gazing across obscure lamplight at the black oblong of the window where the shriek had come. The dishes she'd just removed from the messy dinner table rattled in her freezing hands, shivering with the uncontrollable tremble of her slender body. A precariously balanced glass jittered against the edge of the tray, fell and smashed to the ground. The kitchen door which was supporting her pushed open.

"What was it?" Aunt Lorie chattered. "Veronica! Where—I thought you..."

Veronica writhed, the older woman's delirious fright unexpectedly bring back control over muscles which was briefly paralyzed by the terror of the scream she heard. Lorie Tucker, slim and tall, her thin face ash-colored and twitching, clung to the door jamb.

"I—I do not know." The words rasped Veronica's dry throat. "Someone in the garden. Someone—it—it did not sound like a human."

"The—the garden." The woman's pale lips parted just marginally to let the whispered syllables out. "Hector... I sent Hector... to the well."

"Oh Aunt Lorie!" The exclamation was rebuking. "In the dark! When you know that he can barely see in the sunshine!"

But there was relief in Veronica's voice, also. She now understood the reason for that scream. The feeble old man who was their only servant had fallen, and screamed. That was all it was. That was all it was.

There was no reason for this fear that tore at her, that squeezed her pounding heart. Veronica picked up the lamp from the table, turned, and headed towards the great arched opening at the opposite end of the high-ceilinged, enormous dining hall.

"Veronica!" Aunt Lorie's bony fingers grabbed her biceps, digging in with convulsive strength. "Where do you think you are going?"

"Out to Hector. He could be hurt. I have got to..."

"No!" It was a shaky, nearly voiceless gust of sound. "Please Veronica do not go out there! Do not go out there--in the dark."

"The dark!" Veronica quickly jerked away, exasperatedly. "I am not a scared little girl. The dark doesn't scared me."

She was, though. The moonless darkness out there eerily terrified her. Aunt Lorie had made her fearful of it, a few weeks ago. The way her aunt had insisted on keeping all the windows and doors locked at nightfall; the way she'd stand for several hours just staring out into the sightless gloom—these things had their effect on the girl's nerves. For some reason she started to believe that her aunt expected to see something--terrible happen...

Just yesterday Veronica had told Willie about the strange behavior of Lorie. The guy who adored her and whom she adored, big shouldered, stalwart Willie Lester.

He had laughed, and abruptly a tender sternness had masked his broad- planed face. "Why don't you let me take you away from all this madness, Veronica?" he'd growled. "From this half-mad aunt of yours and this tainted house."

"I cannot, Willie," the girl had sobbed. "Why do you keep asking me? You know I cannot marry you. You know I cannot marry anyone."

"I will keep coming back, and I Will keep asking you till you say yes." How she'd wanted so badly to snuggle into those great arms of his, to feel his lips on hers!

But she had told him to go and had pulled away, and he'd climbed into his roadster and driven away at high speed toward his house in Sandbrook. And she'd gone slowly back to the shadows of Tucker Hall and to the dread that had settled down upon it...

The dim gleam of her lamp could barely fill the massive area of the entry foyer. It fell over the lower steps of a grand staircase, along papered walls whose intricate designs were grey and dull, stopped at the patinaed, murky oak of a gigantic door. Veronica went to the doorway, pulled at its hefty bolt.

Aunt Lorie was standing next to her, plucking fearfully at her sleeve. "Do not open it. For God's sake do not open it."

Veronica throw her shoulder against the old spinstress, shoved her to the side. "Please, Aunt Lorie. You are hysterical. Hector..."

The rusty bolt slide out of its socket, and the heavy door slowly squeaked inward to her pull. The flame from the lamp sent a string of black smoke curling up, flickered, and then burned in the dead atmosphere.

A rotted board in the floor of the wide veranda sagged under Veronica slight weight. The roof-high pilasters facing the house were a row of pale, enormous spectres marching away on either side into obscurity.

A funny, hushed oppression closed in on her, and the strong scent of lush greenery was in her nostrils, tainted with the miasmic breath of the Swamp of Livingston that held the Tucker Estate within the crescent sweep of its own putrescent bog.

Veronica paused for a moment, listening tensely. The night walled in the sector of her weak light, and cold stems of uncared for vegetation crawled over the edge of the verandah.

A sound bubbled up through the sibilant sea of rural quietness, a burbling, liquid moan. Her head jerked to it and it came once again.

"Hector! Where are you, Hector?" Thick- rank leaves took her cry, swallowed it.

Brambles ripped at her dress as she ran fast down the thudding pathway, the thorns from the rosebush slit the skin of her naked arms. Veronica stopped abruptly, her heart pounding fast.

Something that was ahead entered the rim of light, something that was moving. Something that wriggled, distressingly, and then was still.

"Hector!" Veronica could only whisper the name as fear grasped at her larynx. She then made a few hesitant steps forward--and then suddenly her feet went out from under her, sliding in the slippery mud. She rolled, got to her knees quickly.

The lamp had landed miraculously upright in the muck. Its light painted Hector Stone's wrinkled face, twisted and nearly unrecognizable.

His face was drawn into lines of anguish. His torso was a weltering horror of torn overall material purplish with thick, glutinous blood that spilled from a terrible and deep gash split raggedly through his breast.

The memory of a bull-gored farmer she'd seen years back, came to Veronica's fainting mind.

This sharp wound was like that. But there clearly was no bull inside the iron fence Lorie had insisted on erecting across the area, whose tall gate she made a ceremonial of locking at dust. There was no animal of any sort... What then, could have done this?

A bubbling groan pulled her staring gaze back to the tortured countenance. Hector's eyelids were blue, ghastly membranes pulled over the bulging round of his old eyes.

His skin that is seamed was wax-pale with the filming of death. But his blue lips writhed and words came bubbling out slowly.

Veronica bent closer, trembling. Sounds that has no meaning came out of squirming agony. "Goat goatem..." Sounds without words unexpectedly were drowned by a gush of blood. The tormented body arced with a shudder of uttermost anguish, flung over in its final, dreadful convulsion. A lax arm lay still and flopped down in the mud. Hector Stone did not move. Veronica knew he would never move again.

"The goat--the goat man," a wire-edged voice shouted over Veronica's head and shattered into high pitched laughter, into a cacchination utterly insane. "The piper has come for his pay."

Veronica surged to her feet, swung around to face her aunt. Lorie Tucker's head was thrown back. The crazed laugh screeched from her wide open, contorted mouth.

One satin-sleeved arm was thrown out in front of her and a skinny forefinger pointed firmly—not at the shattered body but at something beyond.

Veronica turned and saw a pale, weird shadow the lamplight just reached.

Panic struck at her for a frantic, horrifying moment, and she knew what it was at which the spinstress pointed.

The Pan the wood-god's statue, haunched on hairy goat legs, stem pipes at his grinning mouth. Arch horns protruded out of the touselled disorder of the carved hair. Good God! Horns. Was the stain darkening one of them only moss or...

"The night—," Lorie screamed between peals of crazed laughter--"The night of the Tuckers... it's only us left to pay the piper. We who didn't dance must pay him... The father's sins--"

Veronica could not see the stone pedestal on which Pan squatted. But she knew what her Aunt Lorie meant. There was a rhyme graven into it, a lilting rhyme from over whose deep, angular letters a boyish Willie Lester had once scraped green slime so that they could read:

Dance, ye morning, dance ye midday,
Dance your sunlit hours away.
That soon is told by Lengthening shadows
I am coming back soon to ask my pay.

The old woman's screaming laugh ripped at Veronica's nerves. It was more difficult to endure than the sight of the mutilated body laying at her feet.

The Tuckers had danced. God knew they'd danced! Darren Tucker the second had brought to the heaven the first Darren had carved out of wilderness, drinking deeply and frequently young bloods and complaisant women from the far city. Darren the third, Lorie's father and Veronica's grandsire, had added new and horrible vices to the celebrations of Tucker Hall.

He'd died raving, calling down curses on the fourth Darren, who'd killed the parents of Veronica in a drunken, crazy automobile ride and vanished into the unknown.

"The bill is well-overdue and we have to pay--" Pan seem to be listening to Lorie Tucker's outrageous cries with his cocked head.

He looked amused, with evil lines around his mouth confute his smile, with evil wrinkling his small eyes... Then suddenly Veronica felt like she was going crazy as Lorie.

"Stop it," she cried. "Stop it." Veronica slapped her aunt stingingly across her. "Please stop it."

The jarring laugh cut off, something like motive returned to the woman's gawking eyes. She touched the reddish mark left by the girl's blow on her cheek. "What on earth happened to him?" she said calmly. "Oh, Veronica. What could have done this?"

Veronica tremble. "Gored," she whispered. "A bull..."

Lorie shook her head in fear. "There is no bull anywhere near here. And am sure the gate is not open. Look."

She put her hand to her breast, pulled out a black ribbon through the seam of her blouse. A twined, old key hung on it. "See, I locked it myself, this is the only key and it has been with me all the time."

"But--what then...?" Veronica shuddered and look down at Hector's lifeless body once again. On the ground around the tragic heap soaked by water spilled from the pail he was carrying, by water and by...

She was staring unbelieving at the mire that was trampled. At black mud churned and trampled by feet whose imprints were starkly plain in the light of the lamp set down among them. At sharply defined indentations which were filling with a slow seep of red-tinted moisture.

They were distinctive. They were definitely prints of cloven hooves. Of hooves too small to be a cow's or a bull's. They might have been made by goat feet....

A liquid ripple of shrill melody skirled out of the darkness, jelling her thoughts. It changed into loud laughter—a piercing sound, mocking glee. Such strange laughter as the Pan's pipes might make if Pan were laughing into them.

Something dashed across the light—a small stone smashing into the lamp. Its chimney crashed and darkness blotted out the scene.

"The goat man," Lorie cried. "Oh My God..."

An enormous, formless bulk rushed out of the darkness! Veronica whirled, leaped into a frenzied, desperate run.

She raced up the trail on the wings of great fear. She ran as fast as she could without stopping through dank blackness filled with the tripping tangle of untended vines, with the stinging tangle of untended vines, with the prickling whiplash of unpruned branches.

The breath of a hoarse gasped heavily behind her, and the thud, thud of heavy, chasing feet. Constantly behind her, and closer, closer it get.

The house loomed forward, its frontage vaguely aglow.

Across its porch the obscure form of Lorie flitted, wild arms waving above her head. She disappeared into the wide black maw of the open gateway, and abruptly the dark oblong was narrowing, narrowing...

"No, Don't," Veronica cried. "Do not close it. Do not close the door on me!"

Her frantic feet thumped on wood, the shallow step to the verandah, and then something yanked at her dress from behind. A vicious, bestial howl roared in her ears. A babbling howl of victory.

CHAPTER TWO

A Terrifying Night

The animal force Veronica to a frenzied leap. It took her on the other side of the porch and straight through a small opening left by the closing door.

The rusted lock bolt, metal, slashed her arm, but she squeezed through. Tired and out of breath, she slumped, then she heard the muffled thud of the closing door, the clatter of its bolt, the sound of a hefty bulk against it.

A sound like a Hugh stone thumping against the wood. The pounding on the door shook the house, but the great door stood strong and kept the beast from coming.

"The window, quick, check the window." Lorie cried. "The window in the dining room. The shutter."

Veronica jerked about, staggered to her feet. Into the darkness, she leaped into the great room where they ate, threw herself across the ground to the open window.

Her hand reached for the handle of the shutter that had been put there when the hall was built for safety against Indian attack.

She quickly pulled the handle and yanked it down. Heavy feet pounded outside, and a face stared in at her.

Very small eyes fiercely glittered under a low forehead. She saw dark features, broad-nostrilled, a pointed, straggly beard, and then the blaring metal cut them off from her vision.

Veronica pushed the hooked fastening home, reeled, clutching the sill to keep from falling. She fought madness whirling within her skull, pulled sobbing breaths into her tortured lungs, and ignored the nausea twisting her stomach.

Crazy! She must be going crazy! For she'd once believed horns had projected from the

forehead of that evil countenance. She'd
thought it to be the visage of Pan, come alive.

Pan, malevolent and alive! It was definitely
her nightmare becoming real, the nightmare
which had left her weak and trembling in her
bed.

When she'd been a lonely young child in this
great house with only those two for company—
her dour-visaged aunt--she'd used to pretend
the sculptured god-let was a rollicking
playmate, her own 'boyfriend.'
And her granite-faced grandpa with the
torments of hell blazing in his eyes.
There had been the three of them, when
Willie Lester had come to play with her. Then
had come the grandfather's last, dreadful night,
his shouted atrocities booming through the
hollow emptiness of Tucker Hall, booming
through the locked door behind which she had
cringed, traumatized and scared for her life.
After it was all over, his profane lips were
sealed forever after the old man had shouted
his last curse, Aunt Lorie had come to the
trembling, white-faced fifteen-year old.
Distraught, quivering, she'd told her the history
of her ancestors.

The founder of the line had come here from the sea. He bought the property from one John Livingston for a song, leaving just the worthless swamp to Livingston. He had purchased workmen from far away Providence to erect this mansion. He had married a young girl twenty years his junior, when it was finished. She had died giving birth to his son.

As if in defiance of Fate the first Tucker had smother with all the luxuries the time afforded on his heir.

There had been enough cash to purchase them with, silver and gold money from some cryptic, seemingly inexhaustible shop. Coins of extraterrestrial mintage, some worn, some green and some new.

The men who'd built Tucker Hall settled on Darren Tucker's property. Sandbrook became a thriving community, one of the best.

John Livingston repented of his deal, came asking for compensation. He slowly walked away, after some time, broken in mind and body by that which had been done to him.

The inevitable had happened. Veronica's great grandfather had grown up a profligate and a waster, what a shame.

His son, the man whom Death had just claimed, had exceeded him. And his eldest son brought the house--and had reached the apex of evil.

The last that had been heard of the fourth Darren Tucker, of Veronica's Uncle Darren, was a report of his departure in a speakeasy scuffle on the Bowery of New York. Grandpa had refused to claim the body.

"He said Yoke's Field was too good for him," Lorie had finished. "And that's the way the Tucker line ended. We are the last of the Tucker and the Tucker's heritage must die with us. Children and love are not for us."

Suddenly, it had dawned on Veronica why Lorie had never married. "Oh," she'd sobbed. "Let us go away from here, please. Let us go away from this horrible place."

"We cannot," the woman had replied. "My darling, we can't. Grandpa has willed what is left of the estate and the Hall to us. But that's all there is. We have no money left to survive on. Those who went before us have danced, and we must pay the piper."

It was that very moment Veronica understood why John Livingston had appeared astonishingly during the festivities of the wedding of the second Darren and presented the statue of Pan as a peace offering. A peace offering! He'd mockingly put his curse and his threat on the yard of his enemy. It was his hand that had graven that verse:

Dance, ye morning, dance ye midday,
Dance your sunlit hours away.
That soon is told by Lengthening shadows
I am coming back soon to ask my pay.

When she'd at last cried herself to sleep the dream had first terrified her... The fresh scent of goat-flesh in blackness... An ogling, lustful face close above her own--a man-face which was also the bearded and horned appearance of a goat...

Rough, irresistible hands grabbing her shoulders, pushing her down. A hairy, disgusting hide pressed hard against her skin, whipping her with its shaggy beard...

The following day Veronica, her eyes downcast, white-faced, a slime of evil seeming to her to defile her body, had sent Willie away. He had returned several times over the past three years, and she ignored him over and over again.

Each time she ignored him she would run to her room, crying, blaming the fate that denied true love to her...

A groping rasp along the border of the shutter at which she stared seemed to scrape against the raw edges of her aching nerves.

The crenelated metal bent inward a bit. Veronica glanced agitatedly across the room, looking for a weapon, for anything that may function to put up a futile battle against the dread monster that tried to break in. She found nothing...

The pounding of heavy footsteps pulled her attention back to the window. And slowly, they faded. Had the vicious killer, the--goat man-- given up already? Did the defences of Aunt Lorie's senile mania had erected against him? Perhaps she knew, then, that the--goat man was coming! But How? How could she have known?

He wasn't gone! He was still outside! Veronica turned to the terrifying sound of his probing fingers at the other window across the room. He was circling the house. Trying to find a way in...

The archway to the anteroom filled with light, and Lorie was standing in it. Some-how she had drawn courage, and once again she

28

was prim, gray hair pulled back tightly from a brow whose fine mesh of wrinkles it couldn't smooth, standing straight in shimmering black satin, a high-boned collar poking into the parchment dryness of her pale skin.

The lamp in her hand was steady. But her eyes were disguised. Veronica knew that the curtain hid her fear. Fear that had been an ominous threat for days that was now a reality.

"Veronica! Did...?"

"No. I pulled the shutter down just in time. Aunt Lorie--we must call someone to help us. We cannot remain inside the house with that monster outside."

"Help! How?" The narrow line of her mouth twisted with what might have been a bitter grin. "It's not possible for us to go outside now. The telephone line was taken out last week. They wouldn't let's have a phone without paying for it. Our credit is not great."

"Credit! But you'd money saved up. You sold the last of the silver..."

"And bought food with it. Squandered it on food we'll never get to eat. He will get in...

Veronica... somehow he will find ways to get in. We cannot escape him."

It was not so much what she said that sent shivering thrills up Veronica back; it was her tone, dull, flat, and despairing. Pregnant with the same grim of despair with which she'd once said, "We must never get married. We must die alone and friendless."

"He! What--who's he? Who's the man with the horned head?" She demanded. "You know, Aunt Lorie. You've been waiting for this moment all your life."

A muscle jolted in the sunken, age-white cheek. "I? How on earth should I know? The Tuckers had lots of enemies and many sins. For every sin they committed an enemy is given. Perhaps--a horned head! Have you forgotten your Shakespeare, My child? Have you forgotten that horns on a man's head are the brand of a cuckold?"

A cuckold--the husband of an unfaithful wife. What was the story of Uncle Darren's last escapade before the one that had destroyed him? Of the young woman he'd met in the swamp--the wife of Dale Livingston...?

Dale Livingston! Hector's gasping, incomprehensible message returned. Dale Livingston! Was it that he'd tried to say? Had he been accusing the descendant of Stoddard

Livingston who lived in the swamp that was his legacy, alone and half-mad in some filthy cabin on an island of harder ground? Veronica had never seen him, but...

"Aunt Lorie! I can get Willie to help! The copper on the roof! I will build a fire up there to send signal. Willie will see the flames. He will come..."

"No. It's no use. The roof is not high enough..."

"Yes it is--Aunt Lorie! I have been up there and I could see his house over the trees."

Action, any action, was a relief from dread. Veronica ran into the kitchen, snatched up matches and an armful of firewood. She was out in the foyer again, running up the stairs, through a hallway, up narrow steps. She needed no light, she knew every inch, every corner of the old house. Here was the ladder to the roof.

She pushed the hefty trapdoor open. Wind beat in on her face from the black blanket of a cloud-filled sky. A thunderstorm wind. Her firewood dropped on the roof. Her trembling hands tried to make a tent of the firewood sticks. She fumbled around for the matches in the small pocket of her dress.

The crackle of strong wind-tossed leaves blew towards her, and a curious jabbering like the quick beat of raindrops. But it was not raining. Veronica quickly rose to her feet, ran toward the wall overlooking the great garden. Reached it and leaned over the disintegrating rail. Sharp lightning split the dark clouds, and the tousled brush below was bright with blue glare.

Bright and alive with movement. The jabbering came from down there, the fast scurry of several feet. Another lightning streamer showed.

Veronica knew what made it. Small creatures, Tons of them, were running through the brush, running fast toward the house. Little black creatures. One of them was in the pathway. Veronica gulped. It was an ebony skinned goat, a bearded goat. But there was something incongruous about it. Something weirdly wrong.

Not in its form or the way of its prattling run. In its color. In the color of its hooves and its horns. They weren't gray as a normal goat's should be. They were bright gold. They were gilded... The creature vanished, and the beat of its strange feet came up from the veranda.

She must have been mistaken. Some freak of the fitful lightning had deceived her...

There was another--a female. Its horns, too, shined, indescribably spooky.

Veronica's hands clenched on the rail, her fingers shaking. For a second she could not think, could not move. The strange chasing figure, the murdered man, had made that garden a place of fear.

But it was something other than that now. It was an enclosure visited by an ancient terror, occupied by creatures that were goat-form and yet weren't goats.

Tag ends of quaky legends slipped across her throbbing brain, traditions of whispered horror. They were under her, their hoofs making a little thunder on its rotting planks, filling the verandah of Tucker Hall.

A thunder nearer than the mutter of the storm that is approaching now.

And then, there was another sound. All her life she'd heard it, but this time it parched her with appalling dismay.

The sound of squeaking hinges came up to her--the creak of the opening hinges of the great door. She couldn't be mistaken...

And there were voices. A deep-toned rumble she could not recognize and Lorie's harsh accents... But it could only be the voice of Hector's killer!

Oh God! It'd been Lorie who'd sent old Hector out to his death! It'd been Lorie who shut her out, helpless in the grip of the terror! It'd been Lorie who laughed and had pointed to the veiled prophecy on the base of Pan!

Laughed in the presence of death!

Lorie had waited for it, not with fear but with impatience, she knew all along of the coming of the beast. Lorie had argued against the fire signal Veronica had come up here to set, calling for help. Lorie was opening the door now to let in the beast before Willie could come!

CHAPTER THREE

Red Fury

A Mist of anger wavered before Veronica Tucker's eyes. Lorie Tucker--Aunt Lorie--had known of some terrible retribution descending on Tucker Hall. To save herself she'd offered a sacrifice...

Hector and Veronica. She was making that deal down there, offering her niece, her ward, in exchange for her own security. It was abominable.

Veronica's clenched her fists, she whirled away from the parapet, crying with choked

anger. They would not get away with it. She
went back to the hatchway. She knelt to the fire
she had laid and thrust a flaming match into
the shavings at its base. The firewood caught—

From below came a shrilled scream, a high,
quavering scream, like the last cry we heard
from Hector from the darkness.

But this was not followed by silence. It was
quenched, by a surprising blatting chorus of
goat-cries, and by the skirling laughter of the
Pan pipes.

Veronica forgot her anger. She spun about,
remembering that Aunt Lorie had been a good
mother to her, that Aunt Lorie needed her now.

She caught up a thick cudgel, hurled herself
down the ladder and the stairs, hurtled along
the dark second floor passageway, snatched at
the newel-post of the main stairway to twist
herself to that last broad flight. Then she
stopped, looking down, shaking...

The light shining in through the open door
showed her the foyer floor. It showed her the
golden-horned goats milling around something
on the floor, something terrible, and bloody,
and twisted.

She saw the bronzed, bare back of a man bent
over the gory body of Aunt Lorie. If it was a
man. He had tight curly hair, very hairy. His
haunches--what she could see of them--were

black-furred, shaggy, and foul. His hands, spatulate, hairy, were occupied with the body of the woman on the floor.

"No!" screeched Aunt Lorie. "You will not get it out of me. It's done enough damage already." Her voice was edged with anguish and panic.

Veronica's arm arced up, swept down. The heavy stick flew down through the dark. She heard it crash into the skull of the creature.

Its thud sickened the girl, but the blow that would have dropped an average man only brought a howl from the one below.

He slowly raised up, twisted around. In a flash Veronica saw the same face staring up at her that had glared in through the window. The sharp-chinned, satyr's face.

Were those horns on his forehead or...?

Before she could make sure darkness had smashed in again with a brain-shaking peal of thunder.

It seemed to come in the house and troll up the stairs beneath her. But it was not thunder, it was the feet of Pan's, pounding up the stars, coming up to her.

Veronica whirled, leaped into a frenzied dash for safety. But was there safety in this great house? The roof? If she could get to the roof. Death, any death rather than...

A hole in the carpet caught her heel, flung her down. She sprawled, despair bursting in her brain. She rolled...

The strong smell of goat flesh gusted out of the darkness. Hard-skinned, hands grabbed her shoulders. A hairy, disgusting hide was against her trembling skin. Through the thin material of her dress it flayed her with its roughness...

The sound of thunder faded away. Lightning flashed in through the windows, and the electric lamp which Willie Lester was trying to read dimmed, flared up again. He tossed his book on the floor in rage, open his lank, loose-knit length, and stood on heavy-spraddled legs.

A frown creased his forehead and in his eyes pain slept, pain that had not been long out of them through the years since Veronica Tucker had first told him she was not the woman for him.

"Hell of a thunderstorm coming up," he mumbled in the habit of one who's alone. "If lightning hits that old house..."

Damn it. If Veronica would only get over that silly idea of hers. If she'd just let him take good care of her. From that window he could see clearly the roof of Tucker Hall... About time he got over his childish habit of staring at it for hours, heartsick with love denied... He walked across the room...

He was gazing out into pitch blackness... What the hell! An orange spark splashed the night. It grew brighter and brighter, was unmistakably the flicker of a fire. The only house over there was....Veronica's!

Lester whirled, dash down the stairs. He ran to the 'telephone in the hallway, anxiously twirled its handle to call the firehouse in distant Sandbrook. There was no sound in the receiver. No sound at all. Damnation!

The rickety line was out again. Every time there was a thunderstorm it did that! Willie hurled the worthless cylinder of hard rubber against the wall.

He ran out of the house, leaped into the seat of his rattletrap roadster, breathing a prayer of thankfulness that he had been too lazy to garage it.

The slam of the door, the whir of the starter, the clang of gears and the roar of a hard-pushed motor merged into one incessant sound.

39

Headlights leaped out to snatch a running
ribbon of bumpy road out of the darkness.
Trees that were misshapen, grotesque flicked
by. The world vanished with a detonation of
deafening thunder and lit up again with a
quivering blue glare of lightning.

Underbrush scraped the sides of the flivver.
Boards of a narrow bridge rattled quickly
beneath.

Higgin's foot thumped down on the brake
pedal as a great black opening in the bridge
deck jumped into the glare of his headlights.
The car shrieked, the seat fell underneath
Lester. Checked force pushed him forward. The
windshield of the glass smashed-in.

As wallowing, nauseous blackness stuck him
with piercing pain he though he heard shrill
laughter close-by--skirling laughter...

Foul, lecherous fingers tore at Veronica
Lester dress. A scream of nightmare horror
ripped her throat.

"You demon," Lorie cried from below. "Leave
her alone. I will tell. I will tell if you leave her."

Through retching oblivion that swept in on
her Veronica was vaguely conscious that the
hands were no longer tearing at her. She

crawled--tried to crawl. She was going down, down into nothingness.

Lester combated with unconsciousness, fought it off. He pulled himself out from under the steering wheel. Agonizing pain streaked across his cheek and the salty taste of his own blood was on his lips.

An electrical flicker showed him the grotesquely slanted hood of his car, the crumpled radiator smashed against a heavy board at the other side of the opening in the bridge.

He got out on the running board, crept along it, and dragged himself over the hot metal of the hood. He was now on firm ground. He was running, running madly along a road lit fitfully by sky-rending flashes.

And with him ran dread. He saw, fresh scars of chopped wood that could have been made only by an ax.

That gap wasn't an accident of rotted timbers fallen in. It was done purposely by someone who had intended to block the road to Tucker Hall.

He reached the high iron fence across the Tucker Estate. The turreted shape of the old mansion bulked against the blacker dark of the sky, and small flames f lickered on its roof. Even as he clung, shaken and distrait, to the locked gate they were gone. That's odd, he thought. The fire had put itself out.

And then he recalled that, that roof was of copper, was impermeable to flame. He remembered Veronica's distressed telling of the strange circumstance of the wrecked bridge and her aunt's unaccountable fear.

Good Lord! That fire had been a signal, a desperate call for help. The danger, whatever danger Lorie Tucker had dreaded, had descended upon Tucker Hall! Veronica needed him--and the fence, the locked gate, barred him out.

"Veronica!" he screamed. "Veronica! I am coming. Hold on! I am coming." He backed away, crouched. His leg-muscles uncoiled like coils, hurtled him at the barrier.

His hands gripped the spikes on top. They pierced his hands with tortures. He held on, his biceps broken, swelling, but his lifted foot fumbled for and found the top-rail of the fence. He was over.

He ran through the tangle of the un-kept garden. A pale ghost looming above him was the statue of Pan for which Veronica had taken an inexplicable dislike, after her grandfather died.

That had been part of the unusual change in her that had caused him much grief. He skidded in mud, passed the statue. Fell and his hand grappled into clammy flesh. He rolled away, trembling. A lightning flash and showed him horror!

He was on his feet, reached the veranda, and dash through the open doorway. Good Lord! What on earth had happen here! What evil thing?

As he paused tensely listening, Willie Lester's mouth set into a grim line across his pale face. The musty dead smell of the great house was all around him. Spooky, fitful flashes of light from the lightning of the nearing thunderstorm was the only light in the shrouded, funereal entrance hall.

"Veronica!" he yelled anxiously.

Willie listened to the echoing diminuendo with which the Hugh mansion mocked him. There was no answer, but he sensed something....he sensed some presence here that was dread made palpable, that waited for his burning.

Willie's fists knotted as if to meet an attack, his shirt sleeves tightened over bulging biceps.

And then he saw it, way back in the vague hall; a motionless dark pile, a dark mound.

Stiff-legged and tensed, he moved slowly across the board floor; dreading to scan the limp heap closer yet knowing that he must do so. As he got to the dark form, his cold hand fumbled in his pocket, came out with a wood match. His thumb scraped across the match-head, and a little flame spurted from the splinter. Its light spilled down.

Pent breath popped from between Willie's icy lips in a choked gasp, and the match dropped from his cold fingers--dropped hissing into thick liquid oozing redly from the corpse.

CHAPTER FOUR

Clutch Of The Dead

In silence thick with dread, Horror quivered in deepening darkness. In Willie's temple a heartbeat hammered against the steel band of fear that constricted his forehead, and his hand seemed mittened, clumsy as he fumbled for another match.

Dancing, minute light forced the prowling shadows back a little way. Strangely, even in the cruel death that had come to her, even with her skull smashed in and her thin frame knotted in agony, something of the unbending severity of her spinsterhood still clung to Lorie Tucker.

But on the pale fabric under the woman's skinny neck, on the yellow of her skin, on the cleaned whiteness of the wooden floor all around her, small footprints revealed, the twin ovals of goats' cloven hoofs stamped in blood!

Lester caught the stain of their scent in the stifling air he pulled into his lungs. Goats! What derisive, mocking thing was this? What outside terror had attacked this house? What monster was it that had slain Lorie and Hector? Where was Veronica?

He yelled her name, sprang toward the stairs. His feet pounded up the great staircase, echoed through the menacing, ghostly reaches above. "Veronica!" His yelled, desperate call resounded through emptiness.

He hurried back to the hall entrance astounding, gray despair hiding his working face, cold sweat dripping from it. Veronica was gone, was someplace in the hands of the brutal killer. Veronica was gone...

Lightning framed the doorway in blue glare, vanished. It seemed to the frantic man that the unwelcoming, haunched statue of Pan had been silhouetted there in the opening.

So real the impression was that he crouched to meet it. A putrid, animal-like smell surrounded him, and a hard fist crashed against his shoulder. With appalling swiftness Lester was involved in a tumult of ferocious battle, was fighting for his life with an eerily huge enemy who had some kind of ghoulish weirdness that made Willie's blood run cold within him even as he fought.

The punch of hairy fists, impacting on his bones as though the cushion of his muscle and flesh was stripped away, thumped excruciating pain through him. Willie sidestepped, got home with his own fist, might veritably have been fighting with the stone monument for all the effect it had.

His opponent seemed possessed of supernormal strength, was enormous and gave vent to groaning, animal sounds that tightened its unearthly, fear- inspiring quality. Lester rained useless blows on the atrocious thing that sought his destruction.

Skinned knuckles were the reward of his efforts, and pain that shot up his arms, paralyzed his muscles.

The monster that had come out of the night closed in; implacable, grim. Lester felt shaggy arms wrap around his weakening body, and he was hugged tight to a steel-hard torso.

The Hugh hairy hands that held him, drove the breath from his chest. He heard his tortured spine cracking, his ribs caving in.

He tasted the salt of blood on his lips, his eyes bulged...

The world exploded in a massive bang that devoured Tucker Hall in a coruscation of electricity gone crazy! Fire spurted--was it in his own head? Willie slammed against a papered wall, carommed into a corner. He slid to the wood floor. He knew that the gargoylesque form whose attack had so nearly destroyed him had dashed to the back of the house, had disappeared.

Pungent smoke stung his nostrils.

Willie managed to force himself to his feet, to reel after his late adversary. It was the haunting thought of Veronica that spurred him past the staircase, through the wavering flames of the fire the lightning-flash had set--the thought that this being would lead him to Veronica.

A blank wall confronted Lester, but to his right there was a door. He whirled to it, flung it open. Vivid firelight flared in, lit up wooden, descending steps.

Willie threw himself down the steps, saw a stone-curved cellar receding into shadow, heard the faint echo of a mocking laugh and a grating sound.

Fire-glare set his long shadow dancing on tamped-down ground that showed no trace of any passing. Lightning flicked through a small high window, exposed the cellar from corner to corner, from end to end. It was empty. Undisturbed cobwebs hung from rafters, the years of dust was clotted on gray stones that were its walls.

Willie heard a racking cough. His eyes were streaming. He was knew that smoke was pouring down the stairs behind him, heard the crackle of flames.

He writhed around, saw red firelight rushing ominously through a wafting smoke-cloud. He was caught by the fire, caught down here to be cremated in a raging furnace, to finish with the end of Tucker Hall...

Heat beat on the back of Willie Lester like the breath of a Moloch. The flames hissed, then roared as old wood caught and blazed.

Scraggy fingers, orange and yellow and oddly green, reached for him out of the rolling murk, snatched at him hungrily. Impossible to return up those igneous stairs--and there clearly was no other way out of the cellar. He was cut off, doomed for good!

Lester groaned, dropped, and crawled along the earthen basement-floor on knees and hands, his head low to seek what little clearer air there was down here. He could not breathe. Strength seeped from him. Suffocation would claim him in minutes now. At least he would be unconscious when the raging flames reached him. His head hit against stone, rough stone of the further wall. Willie lay still, gasping for air, despair a heavy weight at his stomach-pit.

The smoke lifted over him, seemed to be drawn upward so as to give him a slightly greater space of moderately clean air to breathe. It was being drawn up! He could see the curl of the stems, their ascending present, recalled the high-placed window.

Some guiding Providence, or just luck, had brought him only beneath it. But that window was beyond his reach ten feet above him and, possibly, too small to allow his passing.

Lester inhaled fresh air, filled his lungs and scrambled to his feet. His clawing fingers found cracks in the masonry, his toes scraped, caught in tiny spaces. In excruciating pain, Lester climbed up the rough wall. His hand found the window-sill, agonizing efforts got his knees onto the narrow ledge.

A crack between the frame and sash gave him time for another breath, but it was smoke-tainted, cut on his chest with its knife-edge stab. A cough tore at his throat. He fought with it, afraid that it might jar him from his weak hold. He felt dirty glass, smashed it, felt the shards cut his fists but did not feel the pain.

The opening pulled smoke, heat, over and around him. Willie shoved his head through, but his shoulders caught. He wriggled. Sharp glass ripped his flesh, his shirt.

The taper of his frame to the waist made the passage easier when his shoulders were through and he was not, was sprawling in dry grass. The fire roared like an angry demon, and continuous thunder answered it.

Lester staggered upright. The weed-grown grounds were glowing with the red glare of the blazing house and the blue flicker of lightning. He sought the statue of Pan.

It was in its usual place. But it seemed to have turned on its pedestal to face him, and its grin to have become a smirk of evil, ogling victory.

The heavens surge into hot flame. The earth shook. Beyond Pan a dark body moved, raised itself over the fence, and vanished into the woods. How on earth did he get out of the cellar and across the yard? Lester trembled.

There was something ungodly about the deformed creature.

He was too weak to climb the iron fence. Memory came to his aid, he found a depression that had served him long ago, wriggled under the barrier.

Dense-knit leaf-ceiling overhead slaked lightning-glimmer; overriding tree trunks blocked the brightness of the fire and impassable pessimism devoured him. But there was the threshing of a heavy body ahead for him to follow, the dull sound of footfalls oddly ponderous.

The footing grew soft. Wetness-drenched soil sucked at Lester's heels. He was, he realized, on the edge of the Swamp of Livingston. That was where the strange thing hopping ahead of him was going. The playground of his boyhood, the lay of land here, was familiar to him as the back of his hand.

The sounds that were guiding him had stopped but he did not need them anymore. There was only one way into the tract of low, soft, wet ground. Foot-wide, covered by rushes and cattails, a single walkway of solid earth wandered across the swamp, spreading to make the island where Dale Livingston's shanty stood.

Dale Livingston! Enlightenment burst on Lester. Dale Livingston, implacable enemy of the Tuckers, was behind this, although though the grotesque shape that had lurched in at him through the Hall's doorway wasn't that of the swamp-dweller.

A furtive sound, a peculiar sensation of hostile eyes watching him from behind, tingled the nape of his neck with fear. Lester whirled. Nothing was there. Nothing but the silent, the twisted bulks of malformed trees, the quiet - shrouded forest.

Overcast, black sky came again into view as the forest thinned at the bleak edge of the swamp. Here was the cairn of rocks that he'd helped to erect as a young boy, to mark the entrance of the walkway. It lay tortuous ahead, but his feet remembered every distorted curve of it.

Willie was tight-faced as he set out on the dangerous path, muscle-ridges lumping along his jaw, his eyelids narrowed to thread like slits. Veronica was on that island just ahead, and the swart-visaged killer who had stolen her for some mad purpose of a depraved mind. Livingston was there... Willie swore between white lips that the devil himself nor Livingston could stand between him and the girl he loved.

The swamp wasn't quiet, threatening — things of scum and slime slithered through it. A bubble plopped in the thick mud, and a tiny creature screeched as quicksand caught it. Willie was in the center of the morass, moving carefully despite his haste, drawing on memory for the path he must tread to avoid foul death waiting on either side.

The shrilly liquid skirling of conduits laughed behind him, changed very quickly to goat-call. Willie began to run, as the quick tapping of tiny hooves came to him from the island ahead. Black against black, a small form rushed out on the causeway.

The flash of lightning lit up the world and Lester saw that the narrow road was filled with black-skinned goats, whose horns and hooves were covered with gold. A sudden, queasy fear struck Lester as he looked at the strange thing, filled him with a sense that powers of darkness were fighting against him for the soul and body of the girl he loved.

The pipes called again, screeching and blurring with a queer madness. The disturbingly ornamented goats went berserk and stampeded toward him when they heard the sound of the Hamelin piping. They piled up, shoving one another from the pathway, as the quicksand and the thick black mud caught them, screaming with almost human agony, screaming till their screeches blubbed into silence.

A dozen of the onrushing little creatures were thrust to muddy death, but the others came on as the skirling of the Pan-pipes crescendoed. They came on, an irresistible influx of golden-horned annihilation that must throw him from the path, into the slow stifling death of the quicksand.

He couldn't stop them, no power on earth could stop them. Demon or man he would have fought on that dangerous ground, would have fought and flung into the quaking swamp, but with these tiny incarnations of a world gone mad, these horned creatures; he was powerless against.

He turned to run, to give passing to them and return after they'd passed--and recoiled as a gargoylesque dark form dashed toward him from the edge of the swamp. The thing that had attacked him in the old house was plunging along the path. It's weird, enormous goat-form was noisome than the swamp; its shaggy arms whirling against the storm-lit sky were like mushroom-coated limbs of a dead tree come to unhallowed life.

Willie's lips grimaced in a snarl of hate, and he lunged to meet with the strange attack. But the momentary halt was deadly. Horns, a hard head, hurled into him from behind, battered him from the causeway. He arced through muggy air, slumped into black mud that geysered as his body splashed into it.

Mud slapped across his face, blinded him, and filled his mouth, his ears and nostrils with stinking mush. Instinct pulled his head up and back, out of the half-liquid slime. Movement drove down his legs, gritty mass of quicksand fastened on his ankles and feet. He was caught in the quicksand, trapped, and fear ripped at his throat.

Pan-pipes laughed at him from above. The woods, trembling beneath the awaiting onslaught of the windstorm, caught up the laughter and thrown it from knotted bole to squirming limb. Clammy coldness whipped across his hand, and slime-born things slithered close around him.

The pipes laughed louder this time, their laughter warbled into goat cry. The small hairy creatures that had encompassed his destruction--those that remained--turned and scampered back to the island, vanished.

Between Willie and the island an entangled goat screamed in anguish. Its scream was sad. The quivering sound came once again.

But this time it wasn't a goat that screamed. It was a woman. It was Veronica! Calling for help!

Veronica was screaming in terror as the goat-man followed his creatures into islands mystery, and Lester only yards away, couldn't help her. The quicksand ran away from beneath his feet like the slow, inevitable ebbing of grains in an hourglass measuring the short space of life left to him. Surface slime chilled his calves, slowly lapped higher.

Veronica's scream stopped short, as if a hairy palm had thudded across her mouth. And the Panpipes laughed on the isle, trilled obscene delight as jelled mud quivered up to the trapped man's slender waist.

CHAPTER FIVE
The Last Of The Tuckers

Jagged blue divide the universe from horizon to horizon, and the riven cosmos collided with a devastating sound.

The surrounding cloud opened and belched its contents. The air was suddenly solid with the cataract, the earth flattened by the downpour. Willie's world was the inexorable clutch of sand and mud around his waist, abdomen, and his legs.

His body pounded with pain and despair.If only, he thought, that lightning had struck the island and killed Veronica, he could die content. Perhaps it had--God grant that it had.

Water swirled around his neck and chest and boiled over his lips.

In seconds now it would be over his nostrils, and that would be the end. Veronica...

The slow creep of the quicksand was halted. The height of the two-foot layer of water covering the swamp was enough to balance its sucking.

But that water would drown him. It was a cleaner death, but death nevertheless.

Something bumped against him. Horns scraped at his side, His finger gripped shaggy hair.

It was a goat, and the creature was moving fast. The water that had been sufficient only to keep Lester from sinking had pulled the creature's legs free of the mud, and the goat was half-swimming, half-running parallel to the causeway.

Willie reached for the ruminant's horns. The goat's forelegs found firmer ground almost at once. It bleated, strongly ahead. That surge was just adequate to pull Willie free of the mire, to drag him, too, to where he could find firm enough foothold for the final effort that released him from the swamp's lethal grip.

Ahead of him was a rain-lashed clearing; but from somewhere came a dim glimmer, and Willie Lester could see the herd of goats bunched against unpainted boards of Livingston's shack.

Above them a thin right angle of yellow light came from within, otherwise cut off by some covering that blanketed the window.

Lester knew he must get to that window, must peer through it. But the goats were right there, their sprinkling would betray his presence. Already they were unsettled, bleating.

A door creaked open on the opposite side of the shack. Small heads tossed, a billy blatted. The herd wheeled, crashed into the woods.

Lester lay close to the muddy, stinking ground waiting for discovery. But the hidden door close again, and no threatening creature loomed around the corner of the dilapidated house. Lester squirmed to it, raised himself to the window.

The slit that was the only aperture for his spying was threadlike, and a little way from it, within, something blocked Willie's vision.

He moved a bit, brought into sight a recumbent head, an unshaven, savage mustached countenance beneath whose leathery skin death-pallor revealed. Willie's brow knitted. This was Dale Livingston. But the man was dead or unconscious. Who then could it be...?

Someone groaned within, groaned with hopeless pain. Willie's scalp tightened. That whimper of anguish came from Veronica, or he'd never heard her voice. His decision was made in an instant. He turned around to get to the doorway of the shack... Something crashed against his head, against the back of his neck, and oblivion swept over his senses.

I tell you I do not know," Veronica was yelling. "I can't tell you something I don't know."

Her distressed voice pulled him out of the darkness and the pain in which he weltered, pulled him up to the sore torture of nerves and torn body. Willie's eyes opened...

Dale Livingston lay motionless on a pallet of rags just under the window that was blinded by a torn quilt. The light from the lamp flickered across Willie's face, giving a semblance of life to it, but the black hilt of a knife jutted from his bloody chest. A twisted man-creature crouched, blocking his view. It moved...

Veronica hung against the wall, her arms straight lines of tensed agony, her wrists bound by rope to rusted spikes driven deep into the wood.

Her beautiful chestnut hair framed a face that was contorted and lined with anguish. Her body writhed--its clean sun-browned curves naked except for a lacy wisp pendent between thighs and waist.

Muscles across her drawn-in abdomen pulsed, and the strained lines of her arms were repeated in the excessive straining of her legs as her toe tips touched the dirty floor.

Quietly, Lester pulled at the ropes that were tied around his ankles that bound his arms to his flanks. His efforts were useless.

An expert hand had knotted them, the hair-covered, long-nailed hand hanging beside a shaggy, oddly formed haunch.

That hand opened and closed as he watched it. Every line of its grotesque owner betrayed evil malevolence incarnate.

The hoarse voice that answered the girl's defiance was animal- like, as bestial as his ghoulish form. "You know, dam you. You know where Lorie hid the Tucker treasure. She opened the door to beg me to go away and then she tricked me, the devil take her rotten soul. It was empty, nothing was under the Pan statue.

If I hadn't killed her I would have made her tell where it is; but I Will get it out of you if I have to beat you and cut every inch of skin from your cursed body."

His other arm jerked into Willie's vision, swishing. It was a whip, a thick whip, made out of corded snake-skin. The cruel lash whistled, cracked across her stretched abdomen. A livid weal oozed blood...

Willie rolled, thumped against the hairy legs of the torturer. The creature staggered. Lester managed to twist his legs around the massive form that fell upon him. It jolted over.

Hard and thick fingers closed on Willie's throat. Willie's breath was cut off. His eyes protruding. Darkness, the darkness of death, swirled slowly around him...

"Do not hurt him Uncle Darren," Veronica cried. "Please don't."

She forgot the agony she was in as she stared at the helpless man on the floor, as she saw Willie's face turn purple, then blacken... And then new horror swamped her as the dead man on the pallet moved. He was rising from the cot...

The corpse's grubby hand jerked upward with a horrifying, mechanical motion, closed on the knife handle sticking out from his chest. As he pulled out the knife, clotted blood spurted on the blade.

The dagger arced through the air, plunged into the back of the killer. Livingston fell on top of the man he had come back from death to kill, and Willie was covered in scarlet blood gushing over him from both squirming forms.

The thunderstorm was over, and a pallid moon looked down on two half-naked bodies, a woman's and a man's, that staggered out of the woods cloaking Livingston's Swamp.

"Livingston was not dead, then," Willie

muttered. "The knife kept the wound it had made closed, and he wasn't dead."

"He was probably conscious for a long time, waiting for the chance you gave him. Oh, Willie, you were so courageous..."

"Never mind that... We can crawl under the fence right here... Back there, you called that— that ugly thing Uncle Darren."

"Yes, he was Uncle Darren, the man we all presumed dead. Do you recall in the newspaper accounts of the fight in which he was supposed to have been killed it spoke of another one who was badly wounded and taken to the hospital unconscious?"

"Yes, I remember."

"That was Darren Tucker. He told me all about it after he heard you shouting out by the gate. But he might as well have been dead, for years. One bullet chipped his skull, depressed the bone that pressed into his brain and wiped out his memory. He was sent to an institution, escaped, and found work as a goatherd not far from here.

"Then he had another injury to his head, and remembered who he was. He said he wrote to Aunt Lorie, about a month ago and told her everything, demanding money to keep quiet.

She replied to tell him there was no money left and he answered that he knew the first Tucker had a fortune hidden somewhere in the house, that he was coming to squeeze the secret out from her lying tongue.

"She did not mention any of this to me, hoping he was bluffing, but he did come. What he suspected was true enough. Lorie knew of the hiding place, in a tunnel from the cellar of the Hall to an exit below the Pan statue..."

"The devil!" Willie interrupted. "That was why he ran when the lightning struck. He was afraid the fire would block him from it."

"Aunt Lorie told him the secret to save me from him. He then carried me away to the cabin in the swamp when he heard your shout. Livingston came in, went for him, and he stabbed him...

"He went out again, to look in the tunnel for the treasure. The blatting of the goats drove me crazy..."

"The goats! What on earth..."

"I imagine his darken mind must have retained some memory of the Pan statue. He trained them to answer his piping and had painted their hooves and their horns. When he returned he brought his goat herd along."

Willie shivered, held Veronica close to him. "Somehow they were the worst of the whole business. There was something very bad about them."

"They were like tiny imps from hell itself... I was scared, bound, alone, not knowing what will happen. And when the storm broke, he burst in the house, frothing at the mouth and raving that Lorie and I had hidden the treasure someplace else. He hung me up, swearing that he would beat and torture me until I told him where it was. I--"

"Do not talk about it anymore my love. It's all over now. The Tuckers are finished--"

Veronica smiled. "You forget, Willie, that I 'm a Tucker."

"As soon as we get to the Reverend Wilkin's house, we'll change your name," Willie looked at her and grinned. "Veronica Lester is a much better name."

Tucker Hall was a frame of burnt logs, of black, soaked coals. But Pan was still on his high pedestal, and the moon seemed to have reached out and touch the inscription with an ethereal, meaningful hand.

People stopped by to read it. Veronica sighed through her tears. "The Tuckers have paid the piper, all right, for all their dancing. There are no more Tuckers."

www.ingramcontent.com/pod-product-compliance
Lightning Source LLC
Chambersburg PA
CBHW071203130626
46555CB00004B/1564